Mini Sagas

Mini Marvels

NORTHERN IRELAND & WALES

First published in Great Britain in 2010 by
Young Writers, Remus House, Coltsfoot Drive,
Peterborough, PE2 9JX
Tel (01733) 890066 Fax (01733) 313524
Website: www.youngwriters.co.uk

Disclaimer
Young Writers has maintained every effort
to publish stories that will not cause offence.
Any stories, events or activities relating to individuals
should be read as fictional pieces and not construed
as real-life character portrayal.

Foreword

Since Young Writers was established in 1990, our aim has been to promote and encourage written creativity amongst children and young adults. By giving aspiring young authors the chance to be published, Young Writers effectively nurtures the creative talents of the next generation, allowing their confidence and writing ability to grow.

With our latest fun competition, *The Adventure Starts Here ...* , secondary school children nationwide were given the tricky challenge of writing a story with a beginning, middle and an end in just fifty words.

The diverse and imaginative range of entries made the selection process a difficult but enjoyable task with stories chosen on the basis of style, expression, flair and technical skill. A fascinating glimpse into the imaginations of the future, we hope you will agree that this entertaining collection is one that will amuse and inspire the whole family.

Contents

The Mini Sagas

Not That Funny!

He was frozen, lying on the floor, covered
in blood. I started to back towards the door.
Suddenly Dad jumped up, I just stared at him,
then I shouted, 'That wasn't funny!'
A ghost flew out of Dad and floated out the
window laughing, 'Ha, ha, ha, ha!'

Abbie McLaughlin (11)
Ballycastle High School, Ballycastle

Humpty-Dumpty

Humpty-Dumpty sat on the very big wall.
Humpty-Dumpty had a ginormous fall. All of the
king's horse and none of the king's men could
not get Humpty up again. All of the strong horses
tried to get him up and alive. Unfortunately poor
Humpty-Dumpty staggered and died.

Shannon Taggart (11)
Ballycastle High School, Ballycastle

The Wakening

She felt the kiss on her lips and wakened with a yawn, without opening her eyes. Unfortunately when she did, the sight in front of her was not a pretty one … 'And who do you think you are?'
'I'm your Prince Charming.'
'Yeah, I don't think so mate!'

Chelsea Graham. (11)
Ballycastle High School, Ballycastle

The Mad Woman

I ran. Behind me, she ran. She got faster and faster. I got tired. She jumped me. I fell over. She grabbed her knife and raised it. She stabbed me, laughing. I woke up. It was a dream. I thought it was over until I saw the knife in me!

Darrian Quigg (12)

Ballycastle High School, Ballycastle

The Lonely Lane

I was walking along the lonely dark lane when I heard a terrifying sound behind me. I stopped and looked but nothing was there. I heard the sound again. I ran but it got me, then it said, 'Hey, your bracelet has fallen off your wrist!' It was my classmate!

Shannon McIntyre (12)
Ballycastle High School, Ballycastle

Chav Princess

She walked into the ballroom; her beautiful dress was twinkling in the light. The prince walked over to her confidently. He took her hand and said in a posh voice, 'I'm ...'
She pulled away and said, 'Listen bruv, I'm not your Cinderella, I'm not going along with this fairy tale!'

Hannah Woolner (12)
Ballycastle High School, Ballycastle

The Funfair

Falling faster and faster, lights flashing all around me. Screams echo loud in my ear, above the shuddering engines and pounding music. My stomach is about to erupt. I'm terrified but then it all stops. Is this the end? Only one question is needed, 'Can I go on it again?'

Evie McBride (12)

Ballycastle High School, Ballycastle

The Mummy

I went to the museum to see the Egyptian mummy. The room was dark. I turned around and was alone. Suddenly the mummy began to move. I opened my mouth to scream and felt a hand on my shoulder.

'Get up; school time,' my mum whispered.

It was a dream.

Vanessa McDonald (12)

Ballycastle High School, Ballycastle

The Mystical Creature

I was walking home from school, listening to music. I kept seeing bushes moving in front of my eyes! I kept walking, thinking about something different. Suddenly it came out of nowhere! It looked at me with its big eyes. I tried to run away but it got me!

Olivia Logan (12)
Ballycastle High School, Ballycastle

The Hurt Dog

There was a dog named Lolly. Lolly was dumped
in a street by her owner. She was lonely and
scared. She did not know this unusual street.
Then a cat came along and attacked Lolly.
Suddenly there were footsteps. It was Lolly's
owner. Lolly was glad and relieved.

Rebecca Hanna (12)

Ballycastle High School, Ballycastle

Untitled

Have you ever thought what it would be like in
an old dead lady's house? Well, I did and it's not
delightful. I opened the creaking door and walked
towards the stairs and it was there. It came
down, step by step. It had an axe, it swung …

Daniel Wilkinson (12)

Ballycastle High School, Ballycastle

The Haunted Woods

It was a cold, dark night; the moon gleamed through the trees. I ran with terror on my face as I dashed through the woods with my revolver. I tripped and fell into a ditch. I quickly got up; I heard something running towards me. I turned around ... *bang!*

Stephen Warke (15)
Ballycastle High School, Ballycastle

My First Step

I stood there staring down, sucking my thumb, swallowing hard. My heart pounding, could I do this? The distance from the ground seemed endless. A sudden surge of braveness came over me. Blushing, beaming, I took my first step … 'Well done Jade,' my mum exclaimed, grabbing me into a hug.

Jade Trafford (15)
Ballycastle High School, Ballycastle

The Final Sprint

I ran until my feet were jelly. I was in a blur, only hearing bellows from the sides. I snapped out of my daze and made a final push. Winning in my grasp, crossed with excitement. Quickest runner in the world!

'Get up!'

I awoke, realising it was a dream.

Neil Carton (15)

Ballycastle High School, Ballycastle

Life's Ending

As the man lay on his deathbed, with the tall opponent leaning over him, knife dripping with red goo, he finally said, 'Why Henry?' And his hand that once was holding onto Henry's shirt, fell to the bed. Then the final curtains rolled back and the claps began.

Tina Taggart (15)
Ballycastle High School, Ballycastle

Truth Or Dare?

They were all looking at her with hopeful eyes.
Will she do it? They thought.
She did it! They all looked horrified as she ate the
rotten fruit. She turned and said, 'Whose go is it
now for truth or dare?'

Chrissie Taggart (15)
Ballycastle High School, Ballycastle

Game Over

My breath caught in my throat as I watched a shadow approach me. I aimed my gun. *Bang!* Too late. I clasped my chest. Trembling, I took my hand away and watched blood dripping from my fingertips. This was it. I was going to die. 'Game over'. My Xbox echoed.

Kirsty Beatty (15)
Ballycastle High School, Ballycastle

Lunchtime

The big lion is growling. I have to stay here quietly. I am sweating a lot. It's been just a few minutes but I feel like this moment will last forever. Finally the school bell rings. I close my books, pack my school bags and quickly run to the canteen.

Robbie Clements (15)
Ballycastle High School, Ballycastle

Screen!

Several dim lights only lit the street, walking,
scared something would happen. Two lights
flickered. Something in the shadows moved.
Suddenly she turned round … *bang!*
Popcorn flew everywhere! The big screen went
black.
'Wow, that was scary!' said Jodie, staring at the
screen as the ending credits appeared.

Rebecca Wilkinson (13)
Ballycastle High School, Ballycastle

Goal!

The whistle blows to start the second half. It is still 0-0. There is an injury in the crowd, the match is stopped.
It's close to full time; the board goes up for stoppage time. Goal! Gem scores. 1-0, he dribbled around the keeper and it's full time. Gem wins!

Jack McGregor (12)
Ballycastle High School, Ballycastle

The Little Runner

I was running, I was nervous, I was scared, I fell.
They looked at me in a funny way. They started
to run after me again with their big bloody hands.
They were going to kill that poor little mouse. It
squealed and ran. I felt sorry for that mouse.

Graeme Christie (12)
Ballycastle High School, Ballycastle

School Goes Bang!

I was in school and I saw a new boy, he had a big bag. I heard a beeping noise. I followed him. He dropped to his knees; he was putting something up on the wall. He smiled and then … *bang!* The school was blown up!

Reece Torrens (12)

Ballycastle High School, Ballycastle

Just Dance

The music pounded in my ears, suddenly it
stopped. I looked down and Sarah was lying on
the floor, unable to get up.
When she came back from the hospital she said,
'I'm unable to dance.'
On stage, waiting for the results. They
announced, 'Just Dance - you've won!'

Hannah Moore (13)
Ballycastle High School, Ballycastle

The Dolphin Saves The Day

Sandy's in trouble, her head is under the water.
Something is surging through the water, it is a
baby dolphin. Sandy is lifted up above the water
by the baby dolphin. The baby goes into the
shallow water where sandy's parents are waiting.
Sandy says, 'Thank you!'

Heather Clarke (12)

Ballycastle High School, Ballycastle

The Voice

Louise lived in an old house which was said to be haunted. She was about to sit her most important exam, excitement and fear coursed through her body.
In bed, the night before, just as she dosed off, she felt something squeeze her hand and whisper, 'It will be alright!'

Alyson Wilkinson (15)
Ballycastle High School, Ballycastle

25

My House

Tom constructed a house with all kinds of sweets, chewy and hard, but must have forgotten that his fat greedy friend had a never-ending love for sweets. He ate the whole house!
They were friends so helped each other build two houses made of gingerbread which they both disliked.

Ryan Jones (14)
Ballycastle High School, Ballycastle

Right To The Roots, Six Feet Under

The man felt the cold blowing against his face; he looked to see endless holes. Standing there in the murky mist, tall shadows surrounded him. He, to his prey, lifted his arm high, *slice!* The blood ran down his hand!

'Ouch, my finger!' gasped the woodsman. 'That's one sharp axe!'

Kristel Kirkpatrick (15)

Ballycastle High School, Ballycastle

Sea Cave Nightmare

I was looking in a sea cave and it was a windy evening. Just one tiny gust of wind hit my back; I fell in the hole and woke up. Sweating, laughing as I realised it was all just a nightmare. I was able to go back to sleep again.

Shannon McAlister (13)
Ballycastle High School, Ballycastle

The Hand Of Hope

Screams and shouts were the only sounds heard.
Rescue teams searched the rubble for hours
as hope disappeared. A child's mother stood
watching with a tear-stained face. Suddenly a
tapping noise started, the search began again.
As the last stone was moved a little girl's hand
reached out …

Leah Cox (13)

Ballycastle High School, Ballycastle

Lost And Confused

I woke in a dark cave. I didn't really know where I
was but I knew I had to get out.
I was searching in the dark when suddenly there
he was. My palms started to sweat and I felt a chill
down my spine. It was my brother's killer!

Joanne McVicker (13)
Ballycastle High School, Ballycastle

Soldier's Nightmare

It was a dark winter's night; it was cold and raining down quite heavily. The sky was being lit up just by the loud and very scary explosion. I was running and running then *bang!* I thought I was hit by a bomb but luckily I woke up in time.

Ryan Brogan (13)
Ballycastle High School, Ballycastle

The Scary Future

It's the year 2028; the world has been devastated by nuclear war. I think I'm the last person on Earth. Everybody has been mutated. I am roaming the wasteland with my rifle. Then it jumps at me, ready to bite!
Suddenly there's a power cut and the Xbox turns off.

Charlie McGrath Hayes (12)
Ballycastle High School, Ballycastle

The Final Frontier

The three men sat on the step, waiting for any sign of movement. They had been in this war for three years and all of them were aching. Jim was taking the corner with the sniper and suddenly twenty soldiers ran at them, shooting. Suddenly their war was over!

Joshua Hutchinson (12)
Ballycastle High School, Ballycastle

In Trouble

Bob was running in fear when he saw Clarke behind him, chasing him with a knife. He ran down an alleyway but at the end of the alley there was a dead end. He panicked and Clarke caught him and said, 'Come to my house at eight o'clock or die!'

Matthew Maxwell (12)

Ballycastle High School, Ballycastle

The Ghostly Staircase

Fred stood at the bottom of the staircase, looking up the stairs. *What could be up there?* he thought as the shadows darted across the hallway at the top of the stairs. He took the first step and they creaked as he walked on them. Just then …

'Bob?'

Jordan Henry (13)
Ballycastle High School, Ballycastle

35

Untitled

It was dark and scary, the vicious dog bared its teeth, it had just seen a predator. The predator saw its chance to attack but it was too slow. The dog was about to attack but then it realised it was its master.

Joshua Small (13)
Ballycastle High School, Ballycastle

The End Of The World

One morning I woke up and sat down to watch TV. The news was on; there was a very big headline. 'The world is going to end!' A large meteorite was heading for Earth and it would destroy the Earth completely. We were all going to die!

James Wilkinson (13)
Ballycastle High School, Ballycastle

Saving Money

'I have saved 70 pence today,' James said to his wife, excited and breathing deeply as he arrived home.

'I followed the bus back and earned 80 pence for us.'

'You stupid fool, you should have followed a taxi! Don't you realise that you could have earned three pounds instead!'

Mark McFadden (12)
Ballycastle High School, Ballycastle

Hiding From The Enemy

I could hear grenades and guns going off, the sound of shouting ringing in my ears. It wasn't right, men out there putting their life on the line and me hiding away. Then I heard someone shout, 'Sergeant Brogan, get out here! This was my moment, should I take it?

Adam Brogan (13)

Ballycastle High School, Ballycastle

39

The Eating Ants

Gerald was standing at the house of his uncle's when he saw ants were walking to the house with two heads! The ants were coming to eat Gerald! Then his aunt stepped in to save the day but Gerald's uncle was nowhere to be seen!

Jeff Purdy (13)
Ballycastle High School, Ballycastle

Windy Day

Walking my dog in the park when he started to bark at the sky, so I looked up … a large shape. I started to run away into the forest. It followed me! The wind was against my face as I turned facing it, I looked up. It was a cloud.

Liisa Adams (13)

Ballycastle High School, Ballycastle

Scary Moment

I was walking my dog through the forest when suddenly I heard noises behind me. My dog started to bark and bark. I turned round, there was a shadow. I started to run faster and faster then I looked again and it was my mum. I had forgotten my purse.

Sarah Rutherford (12)

Ballycastle High School, Ballycastle

Ohh Noooo!

I wake up in a panic, football match today. Look,
my mum has packed my bag! We arrive at the
school. I have to hurry and put on my lucky socks.
Oh no, they're not here. What will I do?
We lost the match. I was never the same again.

Taylor Jones (13)

Ballycastle High School, Ballycastle

Jack And Jill Go On Holiday

One day Jack and Jill decided to go on holiday.
But when they came back they saw a little green
boy in the back garden. It was an alien. Jill was
shocked. Jack went and asked the alien why it
was here. It said it was sent to visit Earth.

Tiffany McConaghie (11)
Ballymoney High School, Ballymoney

Aliens Live On Earth

One day the aliens were down at the beach. All of a sudden there was a *whoosh*. It was the humans; they were still trying to take over Earth.
In the end every alien was dead, the humans had killed them.

Melissa Robinson (12)
Ballymoney High School, Ballymoney

A Bad Holiday

Dad put the bags in the car and off they went. When they got on the plane the pilot said it would be a rough journey. They hit wind. Lucy started to worry. They landed on the sea. No one was hurt. Mum said, 'This is a bad holiday.'

Rebecca Fleming (11)

Ballymoney High School, Ballymoney

When Aliens Invade

One day there were news reports about aliens
invading Manchester. A man called Jimmy, who'd
come back from a war, decided to do something
about it. He took his guns and went to the ship.
He entered the ship and he walked into a trap.
He shot everyone.

Gordon Johnston (12)
Ballymoney High School, Ballymoney

Goldilocks And The Three Bears

Goldilocks went on holiday. The three bears sneaked the keys out of her pocket. The bears went in her house and wrecked everything. Goldilocks came back and saw the keys on the ground. She went in and saw the bears. The bears saw her and locked her out. Sweet revenge!

Sophie McDonald (12)
Ballymoney High School, Ballymoney

Brain-Munchers

Once upon a time a meteorite struck Earth, from it came bugs! They spread across the world, waiting for people to sleep. After they crawled inside a human's ear they ate away all the brain, turning everyone into zombies. That was the end of civilisation as we know it.

Christopher Hall (12)
Ballymoney High School, Ballymoney

All Aboard

Joanne and her family drove up the ramp of the boat. Joanne didn't really like boats and she was scared. When they got onto the deck the sea was really calm and Joanne seemed happy and relaxed. Suddenly, two hours later, a storm arose and the boat tipped over.

Rachael O'Neill (12)

Ballymoney High School, Ballymoney

Alice's Boat Ride

Alice was 18, she had to go out on a boat to find new exotic sea creatures. While Alice was in the boat in the ocean, her boat started to sink. Alice had to jump off it if she wanted to live. There was an island nearby; Alice lived.

Alexandria Hill (12)

Ballymoney High School, Ballymoney

Zombie Apocalypse

Boom! Bob woke up and there was a knock on the door. He opened it. It was Ryan, the next-door neighbour. He said, 'There are people trying to kill me, bite me, they've got my wife and kids!' Then they came in. Bob got his racket and killed them.

Jack Devenney (13)
Ballymoney High School, Ballymoney

What Happens Next?

One day a man, Dr Robert, realised there was
a problem. The problem was the world was
coming to an end. So Dr Robert and his friend
solved the problem and everyone loved them.
But the problem came back, and this time it was
unfixable. What happens next?

Kirby Craig (12)

Ballymoney High School, Ballymoney

The Cat

It is another day in the room. I've been locked
in for three days now. I get no food or fresh air;
I don't know where it is. I'm scared now; I'm
scared that I'll not be let free. Here he comes, the
big killer cat. What will happen now?

Andrew McCurdy (13)
Ballymoney High School, Ballymoney

Locked Up!

It was another day in this horrible room. I didn't have anything to eat. It was hard for me to get out of here; everyone was standing outside having a drink. I was lying in bed; I didn't know what to do. I fell back and fell into a puddle.

Lee Kelly (14)

Ballymoney High School, Ballymoney

The Homeless Man

He stank, he reeked, he followed his usual routine
of speech, 'Spare some change, son?' every time
I walked past. I had it but I was saving for a new
football, but today was different. I saw him asking
two nineteen-year-olds for some money and they
laughed.

Andrew Hamill (13)
Ballymoney High School, Ballymoney

Why?

It's hard forgetting everything that happened that night. The bridge, the car, the forest, how did I survive? I remember Mum and Dad in the car shouting. They didn't know where to go. Then *bang!* The car's off the bridge and in the forest. I got out, they didn't, why?

Alex Hallam (13)
Ballymoney High School, Ballymoney

Little Red Riding Hood Meets Tina Chen And Mikala Boyd

One day Little Red Riding Hood was in the woods when she heard something scream so she went to it. Mikala and Tina were shouting at Jordan because they found his tooth. At Tina's house they saw a boy and said, 'We have found your tooth!' and he ran away.

Jordan Hetherington (13)
Ballymoney High School, Ballymoney

Climbing The Mansion

I was climbing up the stairs of the mansion, it was pitch-black and I could not see a thing. I could hear the tapping of the water falling through the cracks in the roof. I slowly approached the door, shaking with fear inside. The door opened and then ... *bang!*

Dyan Sharkey (14)
Ballymoney High School, Ballymoney

Alien Comes To Earth

I looked up - I saw something in the sky. It was a UFO and an alien came out and started talking to me. His name was Tom and he told me about himself and asked me to come in his UFO and live with him. We lived happily ever after.

Rachael McDonald (13)

Ballymoney High School, Ballymoney

Fairy Tale

Monday night my wee sister's tooth fell out and then she couldn't sleep. I read her a book, Elle fell asleep. The tooth fairy pulled the tooth out from under the pillow, the fairy didn't like that one so she pulled another one out. When Elle woke, she hadn't teeth!

Chelsea Culbertson (13)
Ballymoney High School, Ballymoney

Floor Below

Floor 3 in Royal Hotel on a late Tuesday night.
Kate was in room 5. One night there was a *bang,*
her floor vibrated. *Bang, bang, bang!* It came from
below. As far as Kate knew no one lived there. If
Kate only knew that she hadn't long to live!

Grace Mitchell (13)

Ballymoney High School, Ballymoney

Little Red Riding Hood

One day Little Red Riding Hood had made some buns for her granny. She went in the woods and said to herself, 'Where could that wolf be?' She went on to her granny's house. She saw the wolf through the window. Little Red Riding Hood screamed and ran back home.

Daniel Gamble (13)

Ballymoney High School, Ballymoney

Charlie And The Chocolate Factory

One day Charlie went to a shop. He bought a
chocolate bar. He found a golden ticket.
The next day, he went to the factory. He met Mr
Wonka. He took his grandad with him. There
were a lot of other children. They all lost and
Charlie owned the factory!

Shannon McSeveney (13)

Ballymoney High School, Ballymoney

Creepy Friday

One creepy Friday night I was in the house alone,
Mum was working. Suddenly bright lights filled
the garden and I wondered what was going on.
There was a loud knock at the door, I started
to shake. I looked out - it was my grandad in his
jeep.

Sarah-Louise Leighton (14)
Ballymoney High School, Ballymoney

Lost In Time

I woke up, it was pitch-black but my watch said it was eight o'clock. I went downstairs, I noticed that I was not at home - I was in a war zone. I thought, *how did I get here?* But I was actually on a movie set!

Jason Boal (13)
Ballymoney High School, Ballymoney

Untitled

I was lying in bed one night reading a horror novel
and it was getting very good. The man had just
seen his dead cousin go by his window and then
suddenly his mirror fell off the wall and then so
did mine! Or at least I thought it did …

David McGoldrick (14)

Ballymoney High School, Ballymoney

The Weekly Wash

It was a Sunday, that time of the week. It was wash day. His ma came after him with the scrubber. Stinky Steve was rotten with BO. She threw him into the tub. He was finally clean. That was the BO away for another week!

Michael Duffy (14)

Ballymoney High School, Ballymoney

My Severe Injury

I had been sliced open, blood everywhere. I couldn't help myself from screaming, the pain I was in. It must have been an inch deep! It had happened before but it had never been this bad. It was the worst thing known to mankind - a paper cut.

Gina McBride (13)

Ballymoney High School, Ballymoney

The Bin Brigade

At night they strike, dressed in black, prepared to
nick. They crawl around searching for two wheels
and a hell of a smell. The paper's front page title
was 'The brigade strikes again. Four bins stolen
from men who were on the dole.' Then I saw my
bin was missing …

David McClure (13)
Ballymoney High School, Ballymoney

One Day

It was a nice sunny day so I thought I would go outside with my mates. But my mates couldn't make it so I went up to my mate's house and mucked about for a couple of hours, then my mum rung to say it was time to go home.

Jessica Skelton (13)
Ballymoney High School, Ballymoney

Terrifying Day At The Dentist

I went to the dentist, sat on the dentist's chair
and looked at the bright light and said, 'Ahhh.' I
glanced at his face, smiling, laughing, he looked so
evil. Poking about in my mouth, around my teeth,
talking gibberish.
'It's bad news,' said Mum.
'Oh no, now I'm terrified.'

Julie-Anne Hanna (13)
Ballymoney High School, Ballymoney

Pencil Cases

When I was young I had nightmares about pencil cases. My mum said I was a child! I'd tried to tell her that they were sharp and they had rulers and rubbers on their side and every now and then they had the secret weapon, the compass aka the spear!

Megan Morrison (13)
Ballymoney High School, Ballymoney

73

Aliens

One of the scariest things you can find, nothing
can compare. There are so many and they never
let up. They act so sweet, trying to bluff.
Then suddenly my thought is stopped, one jumps
out at me. Argh! it's an alien, oh no wait, it's just a
teacher.

Anthea Hunter (14)

Ballymoney High School, Ballymoney

The Lion

I ran then slowly crept along the tall thin grass.
Everything went silent as the proud lion hunted
its prey. Suddenly I felt something behind me, I
turned around, it was the lion. I screamed and
shouted with all my might then the lion fell down.
Phew, that was close.

Laura Moore (14)

Ballymoney High School, Ballymoney

Drop, Drop

Drip! Drop! Drip! Drop! Bang! What was there?
Drop! Drop! Drop!
'Mummy, what was that?' I arose from the couch, where was that *bang?* Was I asleep? All I remember was running the bath then watching TV. Really? Could it be? This really can't be! *Sob, sob!*
'Help me!'

Gavin Magee (14)
Ballymoney High School, Ballymoney

Tiny And Bright

Once upon a time I went out to the garden and I saw my bush moving, a ball of light came out. It was a firefly and it wanted me to help, so I did. It took me to the bush it came from and said, 'We need chocolate.'

Courtney Elliott (11)
Ballymoney High School, Ballymoney

Balloons

There once was a girl called Tracy, she loved a big red balloon. She begged her mum, Beth, to get the balloon. Her mum got Tracy the big red balloon and she walked around with it all day until night-time, when her mum heard, *pop!* The balloon burst.

Helen Carton (12)
Ballymoney High School, Ballymoney

It Was A Spooky Night

It was all calm, not an owl flying, not even a
mouse squeaking. There was a boy taking his dog
out for a walk in the dark. Then all of a sudden
there were owls and bats flying and mice running.
An old freaky man jumped out of the bush ...

Sabrina Gage (12)
Ballymoney High School, Ballymoney

Tin Of Sweets

I saw a tin of sweets sitting on the table. I looked
inside and a little green man jumped out and said,
'Hello, my name is Mini Me.'
I said, 'Where did you come from?'
'I came out of the sweets.'
'How did you get in there?'
'That's my home.'

Naomi Murdock (13)
Ballymoney High School, Ballymoney

Long Lost Witch

Once upon a time there was a girl called Chloe, she was a cruel heartless witch who ate everybody's candy. Every night you would hear her laughing extremely loud. Once, on a rainy, thundery day, she passed away. Everybody was extremely happy that she'd passed away, but did she really … ?

Gemma-Leigh Doherty (12)
Ballymoney High School, Ballymoney

Trees

One day I was up a tree, it started to fall on the teacher below. 'Oh no, what do I do?' I shouted. But then I thought the school could be closed so I jumped to another tree. Then it fell. The school is closed for two whole weeks …

Curtis Cauley (12)
Ballymoney High School, Ballymoney

Doomsday

I was going to school when suddenly I heard strange noises, the sky went red and one thousand zombies headed for me. I had nowhere to go. I had a plan to get away from them. I started to panic, nearer and nearer they came, then my friends came!

Jonathan Mitchell (13)
Ballymoney High School, Ballymoney

The Cup Final

It's the cup final. It's make or break for the two teams.
It's the last minute of the game, the team in blue make an attack, the goalkeeper saves it and now the red team are on the attack. They score so they bring the cup back home.

Jamie Hanna (14)
Ballymoney High School, Ballymoney

Freaky Man

My friends and I were down the street, we were coming out of the chippy when suddenly a homeless man started to follow us. We got scared but none of us had the courage to ask the man. The man said, 'It's Daddy!' And then took off his mask.

Kirbie McClenaghan (14)

Ballymoney High School, Ballymoney

85

Two Elves Fighting!

It was a normal day at school. I was in class with my mates. We heard a loud noise. It came from outside. Me and my mates waited and the noise went on and on. So anyway, we did our work. It was lunch time, it was two elves fighting!

Lee Dunbar (13)

Ballymoney High School, Ballymoney

In The Garden

One day, in the garden, there was a big humungous bug. It stared in despair and flew away from me. I ran in to tell my mummy. Then I went out to look and it was back again, I was so, so happy all over again.

Lewis McGowan (12)

Ballymoney High School, Ballymoney

The Bad Night

One night I was walking home just like any other night. I saw someone else running at me; I was scared so I started running. I kept on running as fast as I could but when I looked behind me he was catching up. Then he shot me dead!

Reiss Black (13)
Ballymoney High School, Ballymoney

Don't Judge A Cake By Its Icing

There was once a village in Ireland. When a monster struck the people misunderstood him because he just wanted some sugar for a cake. The cake went bad so he went mad to find ingredients for a cake, so the villagers made one for him. That's a happy monster.

Sam Wright (11)

Ballymoney High School, Ballymoney

The Mouse's Escape

The small mouse was scuttling quickly across the
dirty floorboards; hot on his tail was the cat, the
mouse's worst enemy. The mouse had popped
his head out of his hole, but the cat had seen him.
Finally the cat was in for it, because the dog had
found him.

Liam Merry (12)
Barry Comprehensive School, Barry

Untitled

It was a peaceful day, blossoms blooming,
butterflies hovering and gliding around, it was all
exciting, a bit too exciting.
Evil rose buildings transformed into ashes. As the
life of the town died, the light rose.
A hero emerges! A life is very nearly destroyed,
the hero smites evil …

Iwan Jones (12)
Barry Comprehensive School, Barry

Bullied Shark

There once was a great white shark. This shark was different. This shark was not a nasty shark, this shark liked other little fish and he always used to get bullied by sharks.
Then one day he got bullied so much he committed suicide and all the sharks felt ashamed.

Lewis Plowman (11)
Barry Comprehensive School, Barry

War

The day was Monday. In Iraq the guns were blasting, men were falling. I was running, jumping and shooting trying to find the hostage. But when I arrived, he was dead! I chased down the killer, shot and dived. I went to shoot but … no bullets. I won.

Macauly Steele (12)
Barry Comprehensive School, Barry

Untitled

It was a very beautiful day; I went out to play football with Jim. After about two hours we went to my house and I asked my mum to make us tea. Then we finished tea and I asked my mum if Jim could sleep and she said yes! Thanks!

Billy Rogers (11)

Barry Comprehensive School, Barry

What Will Happen Next?

Amy was a young girl in the house watching the
TV, unaware that she was being watched herself.
She thought she heard something but she told
herself, no! The electric turned off. She was alone,
it was scary, it was dark.
What will happen next? No one knows at all.

Chad Travis (13)

Barry Comprehensive School, Barry

95

All Fried Up

Humpty dumped my tea on the floor; I walked up
to him and pushed him off the wall. I put him in a
frying pan and made scrambled egg. Walked up to
his mother, 'Oops, Humpty's dead!'
His mother tested, 'Ooh, that's nice.'
So I said, 'Put on some rice!'

Lewis McKernan (13)
Barry Comprehensive School, Barry

The Devil Within

He rose in his dark, old, dusty grave ready to put horror upon people. Every night he would haunt those who killed his soul. But one night the Devil saw a very weak victim and instead of killing him, he absorbed him. The old man was never ever seen again.

Adam Owens (13)

Barry Comprehensive School, Barry

The Loch Ness Monster Revisited

Phillip went to visit his friends at Loch Ness. On the second day he went fishing on the lake. After three hours fishing, something tugged on the fishing rod. Phillip quickly reacted and started reeling it in. The monster pulled so hard Phillip fell in, never to be seen again.

Nathan Petch (12)

Barry Comprehensive School, Barry

Handsome And Fretalot

Handsome was an ugly child, he could only have one friend, Fretalot.
Once they came across a house made of Ben and Jerry's cookie dough ice cream, the two fat boys came out.
'Hi, my name is Ben, this is Jerry. Come in!' Ben had a heart attack!

Tristan Jeans (13)
Barry Comprehensive School, Barry

The Haunted

It was a dark, dismal night. It was as black as space outside, not a star in sight. Suddenly the lights went out. There was a splash on the wall. The lights came on and written on the wall in blood was, 'Get out of this place or you'll die!'

Liam Tanner (12)

Barry Comprehensive School, Barry

Untitled

'Mum, the dog has run away again!'
'Go and have a look for him then!'
'Okay.'
Steven ran straight out the door.
'Doogle?'
Bang! Steven turned around, 'Doogle?' A man
ran past him with a gun in his hand, he had a bag.
Steven ran up … 'Nooo!' Doogle was dead.

Scott Alexander Morris (12)
Barry Comprehensive School, Barry

The Small Cub

The adventurous cub was racing through the forest; he was getting chased by the small red leprechaun. The small cub was raised by a dragon and suddenly a fireball flew past Leprechaun Town and burnt it! The cub grew wings and became magical. It grew into an adult.

Louis Deere (11)

Barry Comprehensive School, Barry

The Man Who Wanted To Be His Father ...

Slash! 'You're not my father!'
'I am!' *Slash!*
'My leg! You've sliced if off!'
'That's what happens when you don't wield your
lightsaber properly.'
'How could you?'
'It's how it was meant to be with my twenty-five
inch, dark red lightsaber.'
'Oh yeah? I'm dying. Noo!'
Smack!

Lewys Watkins (12)
Barry Comprehensive School, Barry

Untitled

He sliced into the bloody corpse. He glared into the butcher's shop. He saw a bloody knife. He chopped the body in two with a bloody knife. The boy went into the butcher's, asked him if he had his meat.

'Fresh or raw?'

The boy said, 'Fresh raw.'

Matthew James (12)
Barry Comprehensive School, Barry

The Brave-Hearted Warrior

One bright summer's morning a strong warrior
was walking around in a wood and he was
searching for wealth. He started searching for
wealth three weeks ago. For three weeks he
hadn't found anything except 45 gallon drums.
Suddenly he found a cave with wealth.
He shouted, 'Yes!'

Daniel Jones (12)
Barry Comprehensive School, Barry

105

Untitled

Barry Town vs Barcelona. The dramatic game
began, Messi brought the ball to Henry to score a
peach of goal.
Half-time.
Dramatic final! Barry Town under pressure,
they've gotta score two to win. The half began.
Barry scored a goal! Last minute, goal! Barry
Town won!

Callum Parker (11)
Barry Comprehensive School, Barry

Untitled

Red Riding Hood and Home Dog Wolf are being chased by mad Grandma with a handbag full of sweets. They're being chased down the road and then … an old man jumps out! It is old man Jack. He hits Grandma over the head and she falls.

Matthew Way (12)

Barry Comprehensive School, Barry

The Three Little Chavs

'Yo, let's go to the pub my homies.'
'I'm moving on from you guys. I've got my own
wife and kids and they're better than you guys.'
'I'm going to blow up your house so you die so
you don't visit me!'
'Sorry what I said, guys I'm coming back.'

William Eddy & Lewis Potter (11)
Barry Comprehensive School, Barry

The Hunter And The Tiger!

He sliced, chopped and slashed. *Bang!* The tiger
was lying there, the hunter had killed him!
'Ouch, must be painful, but I'm here to do my
job …
My family, I have brought home and killed a
tiger. We will survive here! Now we should start
making our way, let's go!'

Jordan Davies (12)
Barry Comprehensive School, Barry

Splat Goes The Spider

What's that swooping through the air? Is it a bird?
Is it a plane? No, it's Spider-Man!
'Where is he going?' said the strange man in a
yellow suit with blue stripes.
'Ha! I have a name!' His name's Wolvafine! *Splat!*
Ha! Spider crashed into a wall.

Toby-Joe Fennell
Barry Comprehensive School, Barry

Wolf Pack

A sound filled the air, a murderous, deathly, evil howl. Charlie ran, could he make it out alive? The wolf pounced in front of him, blood dripping from its jaws like a waterfall, red eyes like the gates to Hell. It jumped the wall. Charlie knew this wasn't the end …

Nicholas Thomas Currie (13)

Barry Comprehensive School, Barry

111

The Gingerbread Man

It was a sunny day and there was a gingerbread man cooking in the oven. That man next door was crazy about eating gingerbread men so it wasn't going to be a quiet day, but then, *smash, bang, shake!* That gingerbread man was growing but the man gave a fight!

Corie Mitchell (11)
Barry Comprehensive School, Barry

Conflagration

Embers burned beneath starlit skies and apathetic
planets. Charred wood and stone smouldered
in the frigid air. Sparks danced on the breeze,
winking out as they alighted on the frozen earth.
Two figures emerged from the wreckage, laughing
callously. Inside the ruins, hands grasped smoking
timbers, fighting to find freedom.

Calum Johnston (15)
Brynteg School, Bridgend

Noises In The Night

Tess loved moonlight, she hated the dark. Curled up in her warm bed was bliss. Then the noise started, it happened every night. She pulled her blanket closer. It carried on. Wanting to cry, she left behind her blankets and crept downstairs. It got louder. She let her cat in.

Amy Williams (12)
Brynteg School, Bridgend

Winter's Death

The sun was rising; the snow was falling diamond crisp. The air was quiet. The schools were closed and the children played. Some calm and some so rough. Some children found it funny to put stones in the snowballs they threw, but some knives, children's bodies dropped, still, dead.

Phillip Dowler (14)
Brynteg School, Bridgend

The Dreaded Cutting

She was cutting away pieces of my body, the water dripping down the back of my neck. I saw a face in the corner of my eye and a lot of people's voices. My head was pulled up and there she was. She said, 'Is your hair okay like that?'

Chloe Howells (15)
Brynteg School, Bridgend

The Noise

A shuffling noise was coming from my wardrobe.
Bang! Something had fallen. I walked slowly over
to it, with my arm stretched out. It didn't stop
moving, it got louder and louder. I grabbed the
doorknob. A flying white dove went past. How
did it get there? I smiled.

Jess Holder (14)
Brynteg School, Bridgend

The Game

Jump from step to step anxiously, awaiting the broken steps, I climb higher and higher up the never-ending paper. *Zam!* An alien pops out of nowhere shoot, shoot, die, die, the alien falls. From step to step I climb higher; I am entering the addiction of Doodle Jump.

Nicole Anstie (14)
Brynteg School, Bridgend

The Toy

'No! Leave him alone, you will kill him,' the young child screamed.

'No, it's the only way you will learn to treat me with respect,' said the tormented teenager. He threw the cuddly toy on the floor, splashing into the cold muddy puddle.

'No!' the child screamed, 'He's all wet!'

Mark Cox (14)

Brynteg School, Bridgend

Untitled

Halloween night, scary yet fun to scare kids and
nick their sweeties. It started to feel colder, I
wondered if it was a draught. I opened the door
and went downstairs. It felt colder. I went to the
living room and saw a man - the door closed.
'Please, no!'

Cameron Benn (14)
Brynteg School, Bridgend

Untitled

There were three girls getting bullied. One of the bullies hit two of the victims across the face until the third girl screamed, 'No, don't kill her!' But it was too late. There she was, lying on her back covered in blood, but the bullies felt very guilty then.

Shayll Russell (15)
Brynteg School, Bridgend

The Museum At Night

My footsteps echoed around the long corridor
in the dark. Only the beam of my torch pierced
the darkness. Long shadows stood eerily at me
as I noticed my footsteps again and got worried.
There was nobody there to hear me, was there?
No. Here, I was the night warden.

Matthew Obiako (11)
Cardiff High School, Cardiff

The Fear Of Death

It was right in front of me. I screamed as it tore apart my mother. I could see it coming for me. Its claws flexed as red eyes came to rest on me. I ran out of the living room into the kitchen. That's when I realised I was cornered.

Huw Davies (11)

Cardiff High School, Cardiff

123

The Fall

I was falling, falling, falling. My short life flashed before me. I saw everything through alien eyes, not my own. My sister's birthday. My first day at school. Time seemed to slow down to a bare crawl. More memories. My dog's death. My gran's wedding. Then I hit the water.

Tom Vinestock (12)
Cardiff High School, Cardiff

Jungle Camping

I ran. It was dark, wet, terrifying, all happiness
drawn from within me. It kept chasing, I kept
running, then *grab*. A scream, a shout, too late.
I became a captured victim of the top predator,
the lion. Jungle camping is not what it seems. The
predator roared, 'The champion.'

Sarah Iqbal (14)
Howells School Llandaff, Cardiff

125

The Big Question

What if she says no after having been in a
relationship for two years? I don't understand
why she likes me. It's time. My hands are shaking.
The ring is ready. The speech has been practised
heaps of times in my mind.
'Of course I want to marry you William.'

Annamaria Sgueglia (13)
Howells School Llandaff, Cardiff

Doris Duck's Amazing Adventure

Doris the duck was bored of swimming in her lake. Suddenly a giant bubble rose out of the water. She tried to push it away, but it was too strong and she got sucked inside. She travelled all around the world in the bubble and she was never bored again.

Susie Rendle (12)

Howells School Llandaff, Cardiff

The Fear

Alice knew that she was not supposed to be doing this. If her parents only knew … danger could be lurking around the corner. She had to face her fear though. She was so close … people screaming everywhere, she turned the corner … she paused, screamed and ran. The poor little spider.

Holly Atkinson (13)
Howells School Llandaff, Cardiff

A Taste Of The Afterlife

Huge bright lights turned on, one after another.
It wasn't just me in what seemed a continuous
room. There were many people, staring in one
direction. It was freezing, but I was burning inside.
A man suddenly appeared and said in a dark tone,
'Welcome to the afterlife. Follow me …'

Farhana Tarofdear (13)
Howells School Llandaff, Cardiff

129

Chasing

As I run through the fierce jungle, paws pounding
on the solid ground, I catch sight of my prey.
Pulse pumping, teeth grinding, sweat dripping, I
catch sight of my prey.
Finally I reach my prey. The chocolate bar is in my
reach. It tastes absolutely wonderful!

Hannah Loyns (12)
Howells School Llandaff, Cardiff

The Angry Swarm

A swarm of bees angrily stabbed me as I swatted
and flailed. My legs pounding forward, I frantically
searched for safety. Suddenly a murky pond
appeared ahead of me. *Bees cannot swim;* I
thought hastily and jumped, feet first, into the
water.
Finally I was rid of the angry swarm.

Bella Gould (15)
Howells School Llandaff, Cardiff

Bert The Bee And The Honey Mystery

How Bert longed to be free. He would dream of the days when he'd fly all day and be left alone, but, Bert was forced to slave every day in the hive to make honey and serve the queen bee. However, little did Bert know how soon this would change.

Lucy Jane Dungey (14)
Howells School Llandaff, Cardiff

The Monster

It thundered through the woods, thrashing the trees. I was terrified and my bones shook like a skeleton's. It had long fangs, a fat body, tough legs and was green. I trembled as the monster turned around. It chased me. Its feet thundered down hard on the floor. I collapsed.

Chloe Thomas (11)
Howells School Llandaff, Cardiff

133

The Pet Shop

I walked into the shop, my hands sweating. I'd never done this before. I walked to the counter. Behind it was a big scary man. I looked around me at all of the cages. I gulped and made up my mind. I pointed, 'Sir, please may I have that fish?'

Emily Topping (12)
Howells School Llandaff, Cardiff

The Lost Boy!

Once upon a time there was a little boy who was playing, but got lost. The boy was very scared and started crying.
Two days later a little girl found the boy and took him home. After that they had become best friends forever and they played every day.

Lowri Jones (11)
Howells School Llandaff, Cardiff

135

Over The Edge

You step forward. It's a long way down. Do this wrong and you're dead, literally. You take a deep breath, step over the edge. The ground rushes upwards, then you stop, half a centimetre above the ground. The elastic tightens and you rush back up. Bungee jumping - the coolest ever!

Kristy-Ann Wilson (13)
Howells School Llandaff, Cardiff

The Shadow

'Twas a calm evening, the moon shining high. I
was just heading for my bedroom and turned
on the light - giving a shock to my droopy eyes.
To my surprise I saw a dark shadow. The light
flickered; I heard a door slam … 'Argh!'
It was a big hairy spider!

Georgina Turner (12)
Howells School Llandaff, Cardiff

Walking Surprise!

Vanessa and Archie were walking their dog, Keith, in the field behind their cottage home. It was 6pm and the sun was going down, when they spotted a strange shadow.

'Archie, watch out! Come back. It's a fox!' Vanessa screamed. Archie came back in time but Keith wasn't as lucky.

Ayesha Begum (12)
Howells School Llandaff, Cardiff

The Tornado

There it was, the monstrous tornado, rushing towards us like a racing car speeding to finish. Everyone cried and screamed, nothing could stop this ruthless beast. As I ran with the crowd, I stopped. Seconds later, I tried to run but before I could, I was getting higher and higher …

Salem Yosief (11)
Howells School Llandaff, Cardiff

Don't Judge The Look!

I walked down the street with my hands in my pockets and my head down. I saw a big gang of teen boys glaring at me, wearing deep-black clothes. I was shaking like an earthquake. A boy stopped me and said, 'Do you know where the play centre is?'

Jameelah Abdilahi (11)
Howells School Llandaff, Cardiff

The Mysterious Land

I was so confused and tired; I seemed to be in a
dark room. Then suddenly I heard tiny voices,
they were like little chants being repeated. As
I followed the sound, I realised that I was in a
wood. The noises were actually fairies, but where
was this world?

Bianca Carpanini (11)
Howells School Llandaff, Cardiff

141

The Mighty Gods

The wind howled fiercely. A shiver travelled up my spine. The waves rolled ferociously and the sky rumbled. I was in deep trouble! Poseidon was angry, very angry. I shouldn't have helped Zeus, the core of evil. Now I had to pay the biggest price ever. My life was over.

Zadeiah Campbell-Davies (13)

Howells School Llandaff, Cardiff

The Unsolved Mystery

The wind blows my hair in all different directions.
I sit in a cold, dark place all alone. *But how did I get
here?* I think. I was at home, going to bed, maybe
I'm dreaming. I pinch myself, no, I'm awake. I'm
scared, alone, frightened. I'm going to die.

Anisha Rahman (13)

Howells School Llandaff, Cardiff

143

The Chicken Who Lost His Legs

One summer's day, Mr Chicken walked along the road. He was a happy chappy. Suddenly an old man with one hair on his head jumped out, captured him. The man took off his legs and gobbled them up. Mr Chicken was now legless. He was not a happy chappy.

Sarah Khurshid (13)

Howells School Llandaff, Cardiff

Vampires

Her black hair flowed down her back; her skin was icy cold and white. Her grey eyes were dull looking at Mum, but shining at me. All the girls were identical in this school, clones of their mistress and soon I would be the same. I knew, I really did.

Daniela Harkin (13)
Howells School Llandaff, Cardiff

It Was A Dark, Dark Night

I woke up. *Bang!*
'What's that?' I cried. No one heard me. I could
feel my heart beating. The silence and suspense
hung in the air. My door creaked open. A shadow
cast over me. A monster was lurking. I flicked on
the light and saw … a little white mouse!

Ciara Sampson (12)
Howells School Llandaff, Cardiff

In The Middle Of The Night

She woke up instantly and heard something,
someone was watching her. She looked around
her room where shadowy hands were coming
closer to her. The curtains were flapping back and
forth and she heard the floor creak. She was cold
and shivering and wanted the morning to come.

Jessica Elizabeth Davies (12)
Howells School Llandaff, Cardiff

147

Seas Of Desperation

Mind-numbing cold. That is all I feel, just freezing icy cold. How could I have been so stupid? Stupid risks. Cliff edges and grey mornings of adrenalin. Suddenly I hear a hum, the hum of a helicopter. I am saved! There is light at the end of the tunnel!

Talia Maggs-Rapport (12)
Howells School Llandaff, Cardiff

The Adventure Starts Now!

I'm standing on the dreaded mud monster ground. I can't feel anything. My legs are numb; my nose feels like the monster has bitten it. Two things I feel; one my heart thunderously pounding and the bitter fog covering me with a harsh ripped blanket. I think the adventure's started.

Sharonjeet Kaur (13)
Howells School Llandaff, Cardiff

149

Was It Too Late?

The car came around the corner really fast. It was coming down the straight about 160 miles an hour, so I ducked down and screamed, 'Argh!' It was still coming. I said my last goodbyes but I was OK! It was all projected on the screen. I'm OK.

Lawson Morris (12)
John Beddoes School, Presteigne

The Game

Walking down the street, people dead everywhere, no cops, a red river travelling into the drain, no traffic. I heard a gunshot, *bang, bang, bang!* I carried on walking. Suddenly, oh, game over again!
'Mum, can I have another pound to play the game again please?'

Llewellyn Powell (13)
John Beddoes School, Presteigne

Massacre

The sound of bullets screaming, pleas, but no
mercy, he just mows them down.
'Reload, the police are coming!'
Nervous but the adrenalin was taking over me.
Then suddenly, 'Level completed. Press start for
next mission!'

Ashley Lewis (13)
John Beddoes School, Presteigne

Surprise!

In the dark street, he held the gun towards my face. I stood there waiting for the bang and the blackness to come.

Then the boy spoke, 'Payback!' All of a sudden a splash and a squirt and I was all cold and wet. The boy said, 'Garden hose time!'

Emily Rollings (13)

John Beddoes School, Presteigne

Run For Your Life

Twisting, running, jumping. They're gaining on me. I can see the river, a flash of hope and prepare to jump. I spring, air *whooshes* past me. I hit the ground running, but then hear the most beautiful sound. The hunter falls face down in the river. The deer goes free.

Katy Bennett (13)
John Beddoes School, Presteigne

Issues

We had waited for hours in the dusty, dark, damp
weather. Getting wet and hearing the whining
of the winter wind. We started at the back, now
we are at the front. Waiting for the amazing
experience of it, that people had before. We got
there … we weren't tall enough!

Tyler Isaac (14)
John Beddoes School, Presteigne

155

Dad's Stuck In The Bush Again

I stopped dead still, stared straight into the bush.
Eyes staring back at me. I heard rustling in the
bushes. I took a step back but kept my eyes fixed
on the point. I was ready to run, then Dad came
out and said, 'Help me out son, I'm stuck!'

Tom Lewis (14)

John Beddoes School, Presteigne

The Crab

He watches timidly from behind the rock. He investigates the castle of sand, red pinchers snap, he scuttles sideways. Reaching the castle, stops and stares. He looks at the castle as tall as Big Ben. Next thing, he's taking a swim - little did he know the tide had come in!

Alice Gwatkin (14)
John Beddoes School, Presteigne

What Will We Do Next?

The sun, sea, sound and smells were great. There was a sudden noise. We leapt up! The noise got louder and louder. We ran and ran. There was a sudden *bang!* Dad came through the trees with a hammer. He said, 'I fixed it, let's go home now Son.'

Jack Gillum (13)
John Beddoes School, Presteigne

Hot And Cold

Candace ran screaming as the fire burnt her back.
Two dragons were fighting till death, Ice versus
Fire. Every time they fought the fire melted the
ice but the melted ice put out the fire. They were
evenly matched.
'Argh!' Now can you see why she ran away? I
would!

Samuel Boughton (11)
John Beddoes School, Presteigne

The Chicken Nugget

Once upon a time there was a chicken nugget,
but not any chicken nugget, it had legs, arms,
mouth, eyes, nose.
One day it walked to the city centre of London,
met a cheeseburger with legs, arms, mouth, eyes,
nose. The cheeseburger said, 'Hi,' and ate him in
one gulp.

Owen Williams (12)
John Beddoes School, Presteigne

The Snatched And The Plonked

Swoosh as the chicken runs away from the flying pizza. *Cluck* as the chicken goes into the Welsh valley trying to take cover from the fast pizza. The flying pizza's eyes never stop looking at his soon-to-be dinner. Suddenly the flying pizza flies into a tree and *plonk!*

George Martin (11)

John Beddoes School, Presteigne

Baby Locks And the Three Tedds

Baby Locks skipped down the road, when she stumbled upon a small cottage. Inside there were three pots of porridge.

'Yuck!' she said and walked upstairs. She fell asleep.

'Roar!'

And Baby Locks awoke. 'Argh,' she screamed, jumped out the window, landed on little Tedd's chair and broke it.

Megan Pugh (12)
John Beddoes School, Presteigne

Holiday Adventures

I met a horrible boy. I started being friends with him but I stopped because he was nasty to me. There was a knock at the door, it was him. I said, 'Don't want to play with you!' and he turned to dust. I screamed and ran to my mum.

Charis Brown

John Beddoes School, Presteigne

163

Ghostly Goings-On

The ghost wanted to go somewhere. He went to
see what friends and family were doing.
'I want to go and see Cinderella at the palace.'
'OK, go on then.' They were stopped by the wolf
in the forest. They didn't arrive home.
I'm really worried, where are they?

Ellie Williams (12)
John Beddoes School, Presteigne

Humpty-Dumpty's Fish

One day Humpty-Dumpty went for a walk on the docks when he suddenly saw a big fish on the edge. He bent down but slipped on the fish and fell in along with it! Some boys came along and took Humpty and the fish and had them for tea.

Kira Lloyd-Bithell (11)
John Beddoes School, Presteigne

Untitled

Loriana and Carys set off on a whirlwind tour round the village of Norton where they set their eyes among the treasure chest. Sadly Loriana slipped on a rock at Norton Brooke and died. The evil sheep who ruled Norton got to the chest. It was all over.

Carla Dayas (15)
John Beddoes School, Presteigne

Mary's Pig

Mary had a little pig, its skin as brown as mud.
Everywhere Mary went there was a sudden *thud*.
The pig was fat and plump. When the pig went
through the town, everybody said, 'That pig is
heavy as lead.' So the pig's still fat, so that is that.

William Bartholomew (11)
John Beddoes School, Presteigne

167

The Life And Death Of Cheese

Cheese went into the cave. He wandered around
and bumped into a wooden pole and it fell over.
Cheese called 999 emergency team.
When they arrived Cheese said, 'It was all a
mistake.'
The team said, 'Well, well, well!' and picked
Cheese up and said, 'Let's have him with egg!'

Kodey Williams (11)
John Beddoes School, Presteigne

Ghostly Goings-On!

Lisa was too scared to go to sleep. She saw a
white glow. The air went cold; she felt a chill
running down her spine.
The next day, 'Mum, who lived here before us?'
asked Lisa.
'An old man, he died here.'
Lisa went pale. 'What was that last night?'

Lily-May Banbury-Pugh (11)
John Beddoes School, Presteigne

The Mystery

It was a cold and misty morning. The sun hadn't come up yet. I was having shivers down my backbone. I heard a scream. I ran. I saw it. I was just standing there, petrified. The spooky trees were blocking out all light. It walked towards me and then vanished …

Kieran Lusher (11)
John Beddoes School, Presteigne

The Life Of A Bee

I fly around collecting pollen and making honey. We fly around and sometimes bears chase us but we can't sting them because we die. Oh my gosh, here it comes! It's a bear, it's chasing me. I'm trapped, I have to sting, it can't feel anything! I'm going to die!

Robert Brock (12)
John Beddoes School, Presteigne

Dirty Dancing Mark 2

It all started at a holiday camp where a boy met a girl and was fantastic at dancing. She fell in love with him by having dance lessons with him. They became fond of each other and he got sacked because it was against the rules to love customers.

Laura Turner (15)

John Beddoes School, Presteigne

Brothers And Sister At War

There were two brothers and one sister, all in the war. After the war one brother and one sister were dead.

Three weeks later there was another war but one was still alive after the fifth war.

The tenth war arrived and then he was dead, his parents were unhappy.

Scott Sharp (15)

John Beddoes School, Presteigne

Ghost Horror

Once there was a girl who signed up for a trick she didn't know about. So she went to a haunted house and she was scared. It was a ghost! She went, 'Argh!' She ran and ran, the ghost was coming. She realised it was only a quilt.

Ben Perrin (11)

John Beddoes School, Presteigne

Kitty Surprise

She woke up in the middle of the night and heard something smash downstairs. She went down to see what was going on. She saw a shadow move past her in the corner of her eye and ... it was her cat that knocked the fish bowl over!

Emily Tyler (11)
John Beddoes School, Presteigne

The Scary Surprise

My arms were attached behind my back with
something tied around my forehead. I could not
see. I heard a bang. I thought I was being shot at,
then the blindfold came off and the confetti fell all
around me!

Grace Apperley (13)
John Beddoes School, Presteigne

Broken Dream

My battalion commander lay in my arms.
'Man down!' I yelled in horror as they got closer.
All my squad fell until I was the only one left. I
threw a grenade as hard as possible. The sound
woke me, my bedside lamp in pieces on the floor.
I'm dead.

Ieuan Sparey (12)
John Beddoes School, Presteigne

The Guns

It was a lovely summer's day but all of a sudden two boys with guns were chasing a little boy. The boy thought that he was going to be shot, he was screaming his crazy head off but out of the blue the boys shouted, 'Water fight!'

Lucy Evans (12)
John Beddoes School, Presteigne

The End

She opened her eyes. Lights were flashing,
blinding her. She didn't know what was going on.
Then she saw dead people, guns, blood; ripe, red
blood!
'Argh!' Someone tapped her on the shoulder. She
was too scared to turn around. The end.
'Are you awake? You were asleep all through!'

Millie Cornes (12)

John Beddoes School, Presteigne

Bang!

I was running as fast I could, my enemy was running after me with his gun. My gun was out of ammo. I knew he was going to shoot me. *Bang!* He shot.
Oh well, game over. I suppose I have to go to dinner anyway.

Keelan Shaw (11)
John Beddoes School, Presteigne

Happy Birthday

It started with footsteps going up, then whispers
everywhere. Someone was laughing.
'Let's go, come on, up here.' Suddenly there was
a bright light.
'Go away Mum, I'm trying to sleep.'
They came into the room and said, 'Happy
birthday to you!'
'Ha, ha, very funny Mum.'

Hollie Ann Booth (12)
John Beddoes School, Presteigne

181

Corkscrew

It was pitch-black. In the forest was a girl, lost. She felt sick and didn't quite know what was happening. She heard a rustling noise beside her. It went on and on for about 15 minutes. Then she saw daylight and they said, 'It was a roller coaster ride!'

Kourtney Lea Golder-Wood (12)
John Beddoes School, Presteigne

Disturbing Meal Fright

Darkness swerved! Someone approached me. Was it … ? Blood on the pavements! Lumps were on the ground. Someone was getting nearer; they had a red thing in their hand. I heard movement from their mouth. It was Dad eating fish, chips, Coke and ketchup.

Melissa Bell (11)
John Beddoes School, Presteigne

Gun Run!

I walked out the front door and saw children with guns. As I approached they looked furious. I tried to avoid them but they got closer until I was surrounded by children with guns.

'Take aim, fire!' I felt wet and the children ran off saying, 'Ha, ha, ha, ha!'

Owen Clee (11)
John Beddoes School, Presteigne

The Brave And The Wet

The boy was crouched behind a tree armed with
a gun. He heard someone calling his name. There
was sweat pouring down his face. He ran out of
cover, 'Squirt, squirt!'
'Can't catch me!'

Thomas Hughes (11)

John Beddoes School, Presteigne

What Happens In Wars

We heard planes overhead, me and my trench
partner, my best friend, sat there startled at the
menacing war above our heads. We thought we'd
be safe but in wars you see things happen, like the
boy you grew up with go over the top into land
and not return.

Megan Rowlands (13)
John Beddoes School, Presteigne

April

April 1st came, down the stairs, no one was there. I went to Nan's. No one there. No one in town. I went to the cemetery to see Grandad. The grave was gone! I turned around, a gun was pointing at me. It shot - it was Grandad!

Josh Gardner (11)
John Beddoes School, Presteigne

The Seal's Life

Once there were two happy seals. They played happily while chasing fish to eat. One swam away to live on a rock while the other stayed in the dark blue water. A hungry great white shark quickly ate the seal and disappeared into the deep. The seal was lunch.

Amy Gennis (14)
John Beddoes School, Presteigne

Death

It was my friend's party. His mum came out
with a knife and she shouted, 'Jimmy! Jimmy! I
am going to kill you Jimmy; you're going to die a
painful death!' But when I saw her she asked me if
I wanted some jelly and ice cream.

Jamie Durban (11)
John Beddoes School, Presteigne

Wrath And Resurrection

Passed down the generations, whispered in taverns, tales tell of a disaster. Mountains let fly their pillars of flame and black snow rained. The lands were blanketed, lifeless. Villages crushed, animals wiped out. A great frost descended proclaiming dominion. Unchallenged, untouchable. But, as always, life finds a way, goes on.

Benjamin Thorne (12)
Kings Monkton School, Cardiff

Ghost Town

Perched on top of a bewitching hill stood a charming house, overlooking a ghostly canvas of houses parallel to each other. The moon perched on a single cloud glimmering silver rays over the cobbled road that snaked through the town. A breeze blew as a carriage rode through the town.

Sarah Kearney (13)
St Genevieve's High School, Belfast

The Vampire World!

Sophia was at the edge of the woods. She could sense the presence of Damon with his perfect skin and secretive eyes. He was in a crouched position like a wild animal preying for food. Suddenly he leapt and rested his lips on her neck. Was this the end?

Hannah Rooney (13)
St Genevieve's High School, Belfast

Octoman Takes Force!

There once was a boy called Octoman. He had green, purple and brown tentacles. Octoman was dreaming a dream come true, about being a superhero! Then one day he wished upon a star, *bam!* He fell out of his window and he could fly. Bubble-buster zap-force.

Cara Quinn (12)

St Genevieve's High School, Belfast

Crash!

One fine day there was a crash. I heard it, so I
ran. I saw legs up in the air. The tree was bent
and creaked. Survivors did not move. We picked
them up in panic. They felt sore and unpleasant.
We brought them inside but they were just fine.

Anna McStravick (12)
St Genevieve's High School, Belfast

The Chase

The tiger stalked and watched as the zebra
moved to the waterhole. Its paws clung to the
ground, just waiting. Then it jolted, chasing the
zebra. It twisted and turned through the trees.
The zebra was becoming tired. The tiger had its
meal in the sun.

Hannah Hughes (13)
St Genevieve's High School, Belfast

Lost

In 2004 my dad was going to the shops. When he opened the door my cat ran out. She didn't come back the next day or the day after. We were getting worried. We put signs up. Had anyone seen her? She never came back. We never saw her again.

Ellen Rafferty (12)
St Genevieve's High School, Belfast

Playing Around At Lady Dixon

When I was at Lady Dixon my mum gave me her
watch to play with. I chewed on it then I threw
it away because I didn't like the taste. My mum
came back and started shouting at me but I was a
baby - how was I supposed to know?

Catherine Hamill (11)
St Genevieve's High School, Belfast

The Bang On The Door

'See you later Sophie. Don't answer the door to anyone.' *Bang, bang* went the door, then another bang. Me and Jessy ran upstairs to my room. I started to cry! Who was at the door? Were they going to kill me? Who was it? Wondering, frightened, alone …

Sophie Jones (12)
St Genevieve's High School, Belfast

The Dark Walk

Me and my cousin were walking. We took a short cut through Farmer Jones' backyard. Rumour has it he murdered his wife and buried her somewhere. We heard a loud scream. We made a run for it. I remember looking, seeing a figure in the shed, but I just ran.

Nicole Fusco (11)

St Genevieve's High School, Belfast

The Day I Will Never Forget

One day me and my friends were running about and I banged my arm on the railing, it cut open. At the hospital the nurse said I'd nearly lost the feeling in my arm. I was lucky and just got nine stitches.

Lori Muldoon (12)

St Genevieve's High School, Belfast

Lisa And The Gold Ring

Lisa was in town and she saw an old lady drop her gold ring. Lisa bent down and picked the ring up and chased after the old lady. When Lisa gave her the gold ring back the woman was so happy and she brought Lisa to her house for tea.

Alannah Toner (12)

St Genevieve's High School, Belfast

201

Goodbye

Here I am now, alone and abandoned at the end
of time. I'll explain why. I have a gift unlike anyone
else; I can change the world for better or for
worse. I am unable now to go to Heaven or Hell.
Goodbye.

Amy Magee (12)
St Genevieve's High School, Belfast

The Haunted Hallway

A young reporter was at the house of a young
girl who died weeks ago. On the door it said in
blood: 'All who enter die'. She went in and down
a dark hallway, she heard footsteps behind her
but nobody was there.
The next day she was found dead!

Aoibhinn Loughran (11)
St Genevieve's High School, Belfast

That Time

At about 11 o'clock at night my dog ran down the
street. I was in my pyjamas and my daddy said I
had to go down and get her. I finally got her, she
went to the house but I fell and hurt my knee. I
was OK.

Emer Christie (12)
St Genevieve's High School, Belfast

My Heart At Sea

The day has finally come! My heart is going to sea.
My one true love is leaving me, leaving me with
such pain, loneliness and sadness.
The ship has sailed, drifting out to sea, taking my
heart with it, my love. It is draining all emotions
from me. Goodbye.

Catriona McArdle (13)
St Genevieve's High School, Belfast

When I Was Young

When I was young I loved to play with my sister's toys. I always took her toys because they were fun. We had to share a bedroom. We loved it, playing cooks with our toy kitchen. We always argued who was best.

Rachel Ward (13)
St Genevieve's High School, Belfast

Holiday Mystery

She was there, I told them, they wouldn't listen.
They thought I was crazy. I tried again to tell
them. I saw her running around the pool. They
thought me and my sister were lying.
'You need to find her!' This was the worst holiday
ever! She was never found.

Caitlin Taylor (13)
St Genevieve's High School, Belfast

You're No Friends Of Mine

One day I was walking to my friends. They were playing hide-and-seek, well; at least I thought they were. I walked down and they were laughing and I said, 'What are you doing? Are you my friends?' I was confused; they weren't friendly with me for no reason!

Roisin McFarlane (13)
St Genevieve's High School, Belfast

The Killer Clown

My friends and I were all going to the circus. We
saw a clown staring at us with his big red hair
and green eyes. As we stared at the clown, we
noticed some red blood on his fingers. He came
to us and said, 'Tomorrow night, I will return.'

Ciara Gribben (12)
St Genevieve's High School, Belfast

If I Were A Famous Person

If I were a famous person I would travel all over the world. I would go shopping in Paris. I would have millions of shoes, clothes, dresses, jewellery and handbags, a big mansion, five different types of cars. That's what I would do if I were a famous person.

Rebecca Moreland (12)
St Genevieve's High School, Belfast

The Abandoned Circus

My friends wanted to go into an abandoned circus but I said no because people always say there are clowns there that kill anyone who goes near the circus.

The next morning I was watching the news and it said, 'Three children found dead outside the circus.' It was them!

Niamh Sansome (12)
St Genevieve's High School, Belfast

Killed For A Cookie

Damn it! It's all over! I'll never become queen of the world! Why can't the Devil just take me at the age of 93? I will never again do what I've done my mummy will never forgive me. I stole a cookie from the jar!

Michelle Boyle (13)
St Genevieve's High School, Belfast

To Africa And Back

The only cheetah in Belfast Zoo was totally bored. One day he escaped, sneaked on a plane and headed to Africa. Once he'd landed he raced for the bushes. Then he remembered no one was going to feed him. So he got back onto the plane and gladly went home.

Conor Kelly (13)
St Paul's Junior High School, Lurgan

The Babysitter

Mary was babysitting her siblings when the phone rang. She picked it up and a voice said, 'I'm watching you!' This person called three times when Mary decided to phone the police. They said they would trace the call. When the phone rang again it came from inside the house …

Daniel McCorry (13)
St Paul's Junior High School, Lurgan

Demons

It grabbed my legs as it was being sucked into the portal and its claws dug into my flesh. I tried to shake it off me but my strength wasn't enough and it dragged me with it.
I wake up. My vision is dominated by fuzzy characters … where am I?

Joiel Iqbal (13)
St Paul's Junior High School, Lurgan

Real Teammates!

After the last match King's Youth Football Club didn't like us. They saw me and chased me. My heart was pumping. I was trapped. They pounced on me. My team came and chased off the King's Youth players. My friend pulled me up and said, 'Never leave a mate behind!'

Aaron Rogers (13)

St Paul's Junior High School, Lurgan

Oh No!

On holiday, having great fun, we saw a suspicious-looking man. Suddenly a woman was squealing and the man was running away with a bag. As we chased after him Sean caught the man and tripped him up. Sean grabbed the bag and ran away.

Conor Robinson (13)
St Paul's Junior High School, Lurgan

Wrong Choice

James and Bob were going swimming. Afraid of getting wet they went into an arcade. The boys didn't realise that Jim the bully from school was there. The boys were in trouble. As they tried to make a getaway John, Jim's henchman, grabbed them. Then it all went wrong …

Andrew McGoldrick (13)

St Paul's Junior High School, Lurgan

They Came

They came! The fire from their torches creating an ominous orange glow in the dark sky, casting monster-like silhouettes. Their bloodthirsty roars echoed in gloomy light. We ran. Our lungs burst, our ribs felt like they would rip. Through dark alleys and long streets they came. Still they came …

Joseph McWilliams (13)
St Paul's Junior High School, Lurgan

The Siren's Crescendo

I ducked at the crescendo of the siren, hoping in vain this would somehow protect me from the monsters above. I was wrong to try to escape my old life in the dangerous town where I had once lived. Nowhere was safe from Germany's 'greater good'. Not in these years.

Jason Bunting (12)

St Paul's Junior High School, Lurgan

A Bad Holiday

Johannesburg and Timmy went on a holiday, when they checked into their 40th floor apartment, there was a man with a 12 gauge shotgun. He shot Timmy and threw Johannesburg off the edge. The man was caught soon after and he went to jail.

Christopher Creaney (13)
St Paul's Junior High School, Lurgan

Followed

One bright, sunny Sunday morning I went for a long walk and then I saw a man come up from behind me. I got scared and ran off. I turned around and nobody was there, I looked left and right. I looked at the ground and it was my shadow!

Andrew O'Connor (12)

Sperrin College, Magherafelt

In Your Dreams

It would be the biggest kick of my life if I scored this. The score was 1-12 to 1-12; Tyrone were in their first All-Ireland final for twenty years. I walked up to take the free, I was getting a sore head. I realised it was only a dream.

Niall Callan (11)

Sperrin College, Magherafelt

The Dark House

In the dark house there was a noise here and a noise there. Who could it be? Then a bang which led into shouting saying, 'I'm coming to get you!' Then the stairs started creaking. I opened my eyes and I heard, 'Peek-a-boo, I see you, you're it!'

Calida Crossan (12)
Sperrin College, Magherafelt

The Failed Adventure

My friend invited me to Enniskillen to go on his
jet-ski. We had to leave early.
When we got there we got on the jet-ski. I really
looked forward to this treat - we set off, thinking
of all we could do then, *putt*. We ran out of
petrol!

Nageen Chada (12)
Sperrin College, Magherafelt

The Phobia

I sprinted down the hall looking for an escape and
there was nowhere left. I jumped into the toilet
cubicle. Someone creaked the door open and
walked in. It was a woman. She called my name. I
let out a soft whimper of fear.

'It is only an injection.'

Ross Stewart (14)

Sperrin College, Magherafelt

Tall Scary Men

I was standing in the grass, tall, scary, bloodthirsty men closing in on me. The sweat was pouring off my face; my heart was pounding out of its socket. I didn't know what to do or why they were running at me. Then I realised I had the ball!

Nicola Clay-McNally (13)
Sperrin College, Magherafelt

Carnage

He walked home in despair, the sky darkened
and he thought he'd never feel happiness again.
Just this morning, he'd felt joyful and upbeat,
and hopeful he'd be victorious, but the savage,
merciless carnage he'd just witnessed took no
hostages. Italy beat Ireland thirty to fifteen, he felt
completely sick.

Patrick Maguire (12)
Sperrin College, Magherafelt

A Roller Coaster Ride!

Bang! A left, right, *whoosh,* it was so scary but then, just as I thought it was over, 'Argh!' A crash, a loop, 'I'm gonna die.' Panic rushed through me, sweat pulsed from my face. Then finally, after what seemed like forever, the safety bar lifted, the ride was over.

Mark Turner (12)

Sperrin College, Magherafelt

The Dark Creature

I saw a dark creature behind me as I walked in my door, I ran up the stairs. It opened my door and crept up my corridor. It called out my name weirdly. It finally reached me and turned on the lights. It was my granny holding my woolly jumper.

Erica Simpson (11)
Sperrin College, Magherafelt

Surprise!

Claire walked slowly up the twisting driveway.
She rapped the large wooden door and was
greeted with deathly silence. She set her
quivering hand on the doorknob and sneaked in.
She heard muted laughter from the next room.
Claire tiptoed in, only to be leapt upon!
'Surprise!' her dad shouted.

Luc Roberts (12)
Sperrin College, Magherafelt

Branded

She was walking, lost, in dark woodlands. She saw a small hut. She went inside. The porridge was delicious; the beds comfy. She heard footsteps behind her. As she turned the brand came towards her and slowly burned into her flesh. 'You've been sleeping in my bed,' said the bear.

Kawser Abdulahi (13)

Willows High School, Cardiff

Late Christmas Surprise

It was an early January morning and the excitement was building as the day drew closer. We couldn't wait until he arrived. We were well prepared. Dark eyes looked up at us from black and tan fur. Our late Christmas surprise; a playful Yorkshire terrier puppy called Titch.

Georgia Huntington (12)

Ysgol Dyffryn Nantlle, Penygroes

Jessica's Birthday Surprise

Tall and pretty, Jessica always sucked her thumb.
The fairies decided to give her a present for
her birthday. They turned her thumb into tasty
chocolate. Jessica sucked her thumb away. The
fairies gave her little pink thumb back. She never
sucked her thumb again.

Melissa Lambe (11)
Ysgol Dyffryn Nantlle, Penygroes

My Favourite Day

Butterflies fluttered in my stomach as I grasped
the yellow, pink and orange bowling ball. I
stopped, I looked and I saw the café and my dad.
He looked so proud. I bowled my hardest. At
last my first turkey! The butterflies disappeared. I
stood there happy, surprised and joyful.

Olivia Ann Tym (12)
Ysgol Dyffryn Nantlle, Penygroes

235

Who's The Best?

Tom crouched nervously in the corner. The
creaking door opened and his fear grew. A
massive giant came crashing in, pushing and
shoving the little boy. Tom finally had had enough;
his anger grew like a red mist.
'Leave me alone you bully!'
Shocked, the big giant deflated and disappeared.

Catrin Puetz (14)
Ysgol Gyfun Dyffryn Teifi, Llandysul

The Murder!

The man sneaked up behind his victim, a knife in his hand. The glowing knife flew through the air, slicing into the victim's back. He fell lifeless on the ground. A roar of clapping erupted from the crowd. The actors stood up and took a bow.

Owain Taylor (14)
Ysgol Gyfun Dyffryn Teifi, Llandysul

The Stalker

The girl danced gracefully down dark, gloomy
streets, walking briskly keeping space between
them. She began to feel afraid, the light faded,
it was cold! The pursuer was in the shadow.
She turned a corner and started at the dazzling
sunlight. Turning she saw to her surprise her
shadow.

Mandy Rhiannon Lewis-Gilham (14)
Ysgol Gyfun Dyffryn Teifi, Llandysul

Over The Top

The piercing whistle blew. The men climbed
reluctantly up and over the trenches. They ran.
Bombs exploded wildly in the blood-red sky.
The sound of men screaming shook the air.
They pulled out their guns and *bang!* Then black,
bold writing came up - 'To be continued' - the
programme ended.

Gwyn Aled Rennolf (14)
Ysgol Gyfun Dyffryn Teifi, Llandysul

The Storm

As I stepped out the door I could see the dark clouds looming. The rain was piercing itself against my skin and the thunder was echoing loudly in my ears. The wind was throwing me viciously like a doll, and suddenly it threw me with a *bang* on the floor.

Angharad Gwen Isaac (14)
Ysgol Gyfun Dyffryn Teifi, Llandysul

The Dragon Slayer

I bravely walked up the narrow path to the dragon's mysterious gloomy cavern. There slept the beast unaware of the ruthless dangerous slayer before him. I courageously walked up to the dragon. I was about to slay the savage killer. Suddenly Mum shouted, 'Stop pestering the dog in his kennel!'

Dyfan Rhys Davies (13)
Ysgol Gyfun Dyffryn Teifi, Llandysul

The Game Killer

A mysterious shadow ran after me swiftly,
relentlessly hunting me down in the submarine's
quiet depths. I was the survivor; I hid near the
killing torpedoes. I could hear footsteps coming.
He found me. He pulled the trigger on his
murderous gun.
'William, dinner's ready!'
'Coming.' The game was over.

Peter Gillibrand (13)
Ysgol Gyfun Dyffryn Teifi, Llandysul

The Thief In The House

The thief crept silently around the lair of the
giants. *Hide!* A giant approached. He crept to the
kitchen. On the counter a tempting golden nugget
sparkled. Another giant entered, picked up the
nugget of cheese and ate it. The boy left happy,
the mouse left hungry.

Thomas Jay Jones (13)
Ysgol Gyfun Dyffryn Teifi, Llandysul

243

Storm

The sky turned grey as large clouds loomed over the area. The wind screeched like a bagpipe, shaking and rattling the unfortunate trees. Poor Johnny battled against the wind. The wind pushed, and pushed, and pushed. Johnny lost his footing; he also lost the battle. He landed in the bushes.

Dafydd Bowen (14)
Ysgol Gyfun Dyffryn Teifi, Llandysul

Tricks Of The Dark!

Claire crouched in the shadowed corner of her room. She listened intently into the vast darkness as the floorboards creaked outside her door. Claire held her breath, frozen with fear. The door slowly creaked open, a dark shadowed creature crept towards her.

'Who's there?' Claire cried. Then suddenly …

miaow!

Lauren Davies (14)

Ysgol Gyfun Dyffryn Teifi, Llandysul

Life Or Death

He crept through the long African grass, lying
down near the zebra. He got nearer and nearer.
The chase was on. The lion opened his mouth
ready to suffocate the zebra. The lion leapt. He
had caught the zebra. He was satisfied with his
catch. He ate well that night.

Michael Douglas (13)
Ysgol Gyfun Dyffryn Teifi, Llandysul

What Waited?

It tiptoed through the wild grass, creeping up on its prey, its hunger very great. Its spiked tongue slashed in and out from its slippery mouth. It licked its lips, ready for a meat feast. *Whoosh!* An enormous, reeking dish of cat food waited on the kitchen floor.

Hanna Thomas (14)
Ysgol Gyfun Dyffryn Teifi, Llandysul

247

The King

'It's my castle and she is my princess, don't come any closer.' *Bang! Bang!* The soldiers fired, ready to kill me. Hundreds of them ready to take my castle and princess.

'I am the king.'

'Come on Tom, get off the bouncy castle,' called Mum with a smile.

Ceinwen Lloyd (13)
Ysgol Gyfun Dyffryn Teifi, Llandysul

Stalking Seattle

Threatening clouds were looming, waiting to explode, so was Albert. Parched with thirst, he stalked Seattle for human blood. Pouncing on his prey, he ripped through flesh with glistening fangs. Everything came to a stop. Clouds moved swiftly away to torment their next destination and Albert to his next victim.

Shannon Rowlands (14)
Ysgol Gyfun Dyffryn Teifi, Llandysul

The Beast

Slowly the beast crept close, with not so much as a creak on the wooden floor. With its large green eyes focused solely on its prey, it slipped closer. It stopped with a jerk and prepared for the pounce. It jumped! But the prey caught it.
'Kitty, there you are!'

Robin Samuel Franks (14)
Ysgol Gyfun Dyffryn Teifi, Llandysul

The Stalking Of Jack The Ripper

Down dark and murky streets she danced alone.
Danger stirred deep inside the broadening
shadows. Like a cat he padded noiselessly after
her. Like a spring the snake coiled, a knife smirked
in his hand. Turning slowly she laughed. Gleaming
vampire fangs flashed briefly; Jack the Ripper was
no more.

Fleur Snow (13)

Ysgol Gyfun Dyffryn Teifi, Llandysul

251

The Silent Stalker

The silent stalker, always present. It sneaks up on me when I least expect it. During daylight hours it hides behind me. As night falls, I catch a glimpse as I pass beneath the street light. It mirrors my movements before disappearing into the darkness. My shadow is always there.

Alice Walters (13)

Ysgol Gyfun Dyffryn Teifi, Llandysul

Sniper Fight

I was last, a lone-wolf, a ghost lurking, searching for the sniper. I had seconds to get to the HQ. It was in sight, I gazed at the distance, glanced at the sniper. We stared at each other; it was first to the trigger. *Bang!* Tango down. *Game over.*

Christian Price (13)
Ysgol Gyfun Dyffryn Teifi, Llandysul

The Great Chase

He ran as fast as he could down the dark alleyways with a big sack of money on his back. He couldn't run much further, there was nowhere to go. A dead end. Policemen were right behind him.
The theme of the soap came on and we sighed in relief.

Manon Thomas (13)
Ysgol Gyfun Dyffryn Teifi, Llandysul

The Shadow

An enormous terrifying shadow crept forwards towards me. The moon glowed mysteriously. Fierce yellow eyes came frighteningly closer. There was no sound. I could feel the silence. The alley began to close in on me. I shrank back slowly, then it appeared; the black cat from next door.

Carys Jones (13)
Ysgol Gyfun Dyffryn Teifi, Llandysul

Information

We hope you have enjoyed reading this book - and that you will continue to enjoy it in the coming years.

If you like reading and writing, drop us a line or give us a call and we'll send you a free information pack. Alternatively visit our website at **www.youngwriters.co.uk**

Write to:

Young Writers Information,
Remus House,
Coltsfoot Drive,
Peterborough,
PE2 9JX

Tel: (01733) 890066
Email: youngwriters@forwardpress.co.uk